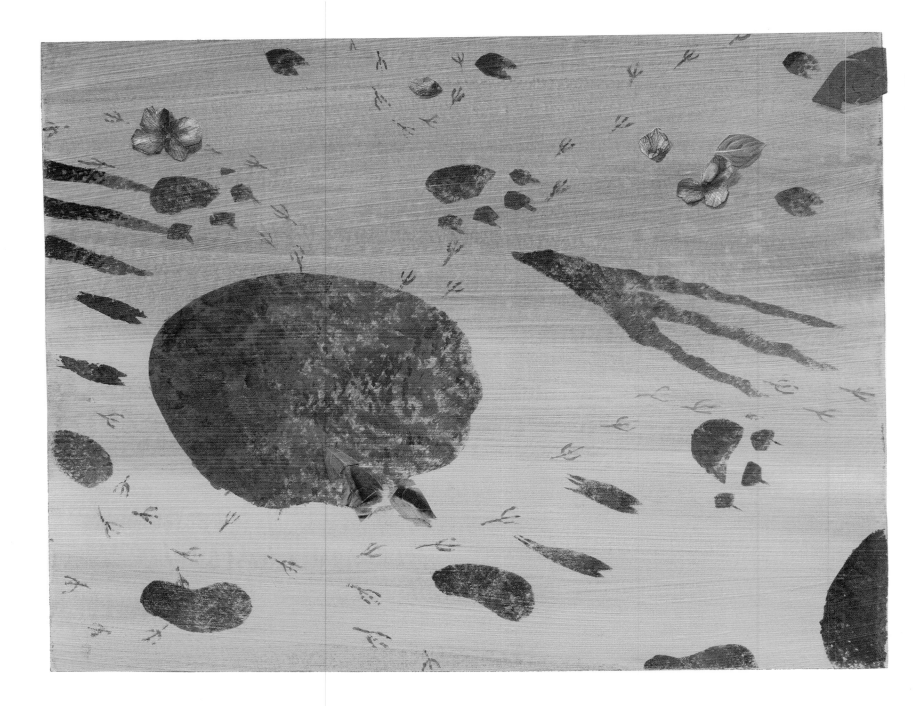

# The Carnival of the Animals

Music by CAMILLE SAINT-SAËNS

New verses by JACK PRELUTSKY • Illustrated by MARY GRANDPRÉ

with a fully orchestrated CD of the Camille Saint-Saëns music

ALFRED A. KNOPF  NEW YORK

## Introduction

Welcome to our carnival,
Where birds and beasts and such
Behave a lot like people do,
At times a bit too much.

You'll meet the regal lion
And the captivating swan,
The irritating donkeys
That prattle on and on.

You'll meet a tortoise, and some fish
With undulating fins.
Welcome to our carnival—
The music now begins.

## The Lion

It's evident the lion is king,
In charge of almost everything.
Avoid the beast at any cost,
For if you fail, then all is lost.
If you should hear the lion cough,
Don't hesitate to hurry off,
And if you hear his frightful roars,
Remove yourself to distant shores.

The lordly lion longs to sup
On living prey, and chew it up.
Try not to fall within his sight,
Lest he dispatch you, bite by bite.
Besides his royal magnificence,
The lion possesses common sense,
And manages to labor less
Than every lovely lioness.

## Rooster and Hens

The hens all rush around the yard,
They hurry hurry hurry.
They peck peck peck and cluck cluck cluck,
They scurry scurry scurry.
They fuss and fret and fret and fuss
With feathers in a flurry,
Until they rest upon their nest
And cease their senseless worry.

The hens each lay a single egg,
Then sit on it, contented.
The rooster treats this news as though
It were unprecedented.
With puffed-up chest, he crows and crows
Till he appears demented.
He seems to think a chicken egg
Was something he invented.

## The Donkeys of the Wild

They haven't any manners,
And they haven't any sense.
There's not a word that anyone
Can say in their defense.

Their ways are so unsavory
They'll never get ahead.
They are the donkeys of the wild—
That's all that need be said.

## The Tortoise

The tortoise lugs his house about
And lumbers on all fours.
He clearly never seems to be
Completely out-of-doors.
The tortoise is a cautious sort,
Not known for being bold,
And so the tortoise lives to be
Exceptionally old.

The tortoise never hurries
And is happily resigned
To being late for dinner
And to being left behind.
The tortoise doesn't ask for more
If he can do with less—
Perhaps that is the secret
Of the tortoise's success.

# Elephants

An elephant never forgets to remember
The things he remembers to never forget.
An elephant knows that it snows in December,
That summer is warmer and water is wet.

An elephant's ears are a genuine wonder,
An elephant's trunk is an elephant's pride.
His footfalls are often mistaken for thunder—
If you're in the neighborhood, do step aside.

When elephants gather, the ground starts to tremble
Beneath the great weight of their ponderous feet.
Be glad there are elephants left to assemble—
Without them our planet would feel incomplete.

## Kangaroos

This fact is essential about kangaroos—
They hop energetically, just as they choose.
They hop over rocks, over fences and streams,
And probably hop in their kangaroo dreams.

When they aren't sleeping or swallowing food,
They hop and they hop as though being pursued,
For hopping's an action they cannot refuse—
This fact is essential about kangaroos.

## Aquarium

In a tank filled to the brim,
Little fishes slowly swim
Endlessly from place to place,
Rarely varying their pace.

There is little that they know.
They blow kisses as they go.
They don't notice what they see,
Or their own monotony.

Each one has no other wish
Than to be a little fish
Neither jubilant nor glum
In a small aquarium.

## Personages with Long Ears

They love to loudly bray and bray,
And bray away both night and day.
Determined that their brays be heard,
They're both obnoxious and absurd.

They bray when it is calm and warm,
They bray throughout a raging storm.
To fill the world with coarse hee-haws
(Sometimes without the briefest pause)
Appears to be their only cause.

# The Cuckoo

Oh cuckoo, cuckoo, cuckoo,
We must number you among
Those creatures with no interest
In parenting their young.

You slyly lay your egg within
Some smaller bird's abode,
Thus demonstrating that you lack
The slightest moral code.

Oh cuckoo, cuckoo, cuckoo,
It's no wonder you're reviled,
Permitting that unwitting bird
To cultivate your child.

# Birds

They flitter here,
They flitter there,
Enjoying every breeze,
And twitter songs of happiness
Amid the sheltering trees.

They build their nests,
They hatch their eggs,
They warble as they thrive.
With every note they tell the world
It's good to be alive.

## Pianists

Practice! Practice! Practice!
Our piano teacher screeches.
We practice, practice, practice,
But we can't play what she teaches.

Although we try our very best
On every single scale,
We always seem to fumble,
And our little fingers fail.

But we practice, practice, practice
As she screeches, screeches, screeches.
And if we keep on practicing,
We'll soon play what she teaches.

## Fossils

Fossils, you entirely lack
The basic knack of coming back,
For, fossils, you're extinct, and so
There's nowhere left for you to go.

Poor fossils, long without a skin,
Today you simply don't fit in.
One wonders if you were surprised
To find that you'd been fossilized.

## The Swan

The stately and beguiling swan
Glides slowly on the lake,
With little but a ripple
In her evanescent wake.
Although she has no song to sing,
No words that she can say,
She's perfectly exquisite
In her aqueous ballet.

The swan is grand and glorious,
She's poised at every turn,
Epitomizing elegance
No other bird can learn.
Though some may say she's just a swan
And fairly commonplace,
She's positively nonpareil
At demonstrating grace.

## Finale

Our carnival is ending soon,
As all things must in time.
The music's almost over—
We approach the final rhyme.
In moments all the animals
Will take their parting bow.
We hope you'll visit us again,
But say farewell for now.

## A Note to Parents and Teachers

A versatile musician and prolific composer, Camille Saint-Saëns wrote the captivating *The Carnival of the Animals* in 1886. Since then it has been widely used to introduce children to classical music.

Saint-Saëns was born in Paris in 1835. He began piano lessons at the age of three and was soon amazing audiences with his virtuosity. At thirteen he became an organ student at the Paris Conservatoire and also began his career as a serious composer. His opera *Samson and Delilah* was a triumph in Paris in 1890. In his long life, he composed over three hundred works and was the first major composer to write music for the cinema.

*The Carnival of the Animals* is a set of orchestral character pieces, each describing a particular animal. Saint-Saëns allowed the composition to be performed only twice in his lifetime (once publicly and once privately for his close friend Franz Liszt). Because it was written with humor and was most likely a parody of the all-too-human characteristics of his friends, he feared that this work might hurt his reputation as a serious composer. Only one of the pieces, "The Swan," was published before his death in 1921.

As a music educator for forty years, I believe that this edition, with all-new verses by America's first Children's Poet Laureate, Jack Prelutsky, and beautiful illustrations by Mary GrandPré, makes Saint-Saëns's charming composition all the more appealing to children.

Kindergarten-age children will move with the rhythm of the music, imitating the animals. They'll walk like an elephant, swim like a fish, march like a lion, hop like a kangaroo, and so on.

With increased musical awareness, the older child will begin to hear and identify the various instruments used to exemplify the animals. He or she might also recognize familiar themes by other composers that Saint-Saëns has incorporated: "Can Can" from Offenbach's *Orpheus in the Underworld* in the tortoise's piece and "Dance of the Sylphs" from Berlioz's *The Damnation of Faust* in the elephant's piece.

An exciting project for the older child would be to think of a favorite animal not included in Saint-Saëns's selections, compose a simple melody, write a verse, and paint a picture reflecting his or her own creative talents, inspired by this joyful work.

Because the imagination is so important to the growth of a child, it is our responsibility to provide activities worthy of imagination. May this book and CD, with *The Carnival of the Animals* performed by the critically acclaimed Württemberg Chamber Orchestra, help fulfill this ideal.

Judith Bachleitner
Head of the Music Department
Rudolf Steiner School
New York City

*For Chauni and Bill*
—J.P.

*For the Hawk-a-bird, Badger Pete and Dad*
—M.G.

THIS IS A BORZOI BOOK PUBLISHED BY ALFRED A. KNOPF

Text copyright © 2010 by Jack Prelutsky
Illustrations copyright © 2010 by Mary GrandPré

Orchestral recording of Camille Saint-Saëns's *The Carnival of the Animals* by the Württemberg Chamber Orchestra, with pianists Marylene Dosse and Annie Petit and conductor Jörg Faerber, reproduced with permission.

All rights reserved. Published in the United States by Alfred A. Knopf, an imprint of Random House Children's Books, a division of Random House, Inc., 1745 Broadway, New York, NY 10019.

Knopf, Borzoi Books, and the colophon are registered trademarks of Random House, Inc.

Visit us on the Web! www.randomhouse.com/kids

Educators and librarians, for a variety of teaching tools, visit us at www.randomhouse.com/teachers

*Library of Congress Cataloging-in-Publication Data*
Prelutsky, Jack.
The carnival of the animals by Camille Saint-Saëns : new verses by Jack Prelutsky / illustrated by Mary GrandPré. — 1st ed.
p.   cm.
Verses inspired by Camille Saint-Saëns' The carnival of the animals, accompanied by orchestral recording of the musical suite
ISBN 978-0-375-86458-2 (trade) —
ISBN 978-0-375-96458-9 (lib. bdg.)
1. Animals—Juvenile poetry. 2. Children's poetry, American.
I. GrandPré, Mary, ill. II. Title.
PS3566.R36C37 2010
811'.54—dc22
2009008734

The illustrations in this book were created using acrylic paint and paper collage on board.

MANUFACTURED IN CHINA

August 2010
10  9  8  7  6  5
First Edition